Make Me Take It from You
erotic poems and short stories

By
HL37

Thank You Trixie
"have I told you how much I adore you yet today?...

Special Thanks

To Drew Sera, without your support *"this bitch would never have been put to bed."*
Please visit her at drewsera.wordpress.com or follow on Facebook at Drew Sera or Drew Sera Books. You can connect with Drew Sera via email at drewserabooks@gmail.com.

For more information about Depraved Eros, the photographer for the cover art, please visit depravederos.com or follow on Facebook at Depraved Eros. You can email Depraved Eros at de@depravederos.com.

contents

poetry and prose

themed writing

short stories

evidence

mark me
that's what she said
mark me
the way that only you
can
brand my skin with
your sadistic
loving hands to
leave me as
a crime scene
your fingerprints
rose tattoos
on my flesh with
DNA so deeply embedded
within me that
there will be no
distinction of where
you begin and
I end

who does this belong to

somehow
they had arrived at this point
their bodies
aching to merge further
limbs twisted together

her sweat soaked hair stuck to the side of his face
as she nuzzled deep into his neck
his hand gently placed between her breasts to feel
her still pounding heart

who does this belong to
he asked as he pushed his hand firmly against her
flesh

with a whisper of relief,
she responded
it belongs to you Daddy

safe harbor for the troubles of your day

offer me your vulnerability,
and I will return it transformed into strength...

I will hold your breath

whisper I need you into my ear
I will hold your breath

look into my eyes and sigh
I will hold your breath

place your mouth gently against mine
I will hold your breath

kiss my shoulder as I bring you near
I will hold your breath

rake your fingers across my chest
I will hold your breath

lay back as I suckle your flower
I will hold your breath

moan like heaven is breaking
I will hold your breath

cry from our grandeur revealed
I will hold your breath

a twisted form of providence

fistful of hair
guiding you like a marionette
trussed up tight from stem to stern
steel so cold as it slides
give it to me
that from the soul moan like rocks breaking

your uncontrollable wails
when tipping point reached
walls coming down
though not long enough for my tastes

the muffled purr that emanates
when my arm is around you throat
fingers shoved deep inside you
your hand slapping my thigh
as if you wanted me to stop

a twisted form of providence I suppose
all things being equal with the quality and state of
our being

I am not innocent
you are not innocent
no one is innocent

content

her mascara ran in streaks down her face
lipstick smeared across her alabaster cheeks
like a porcelain doll that had been flung around
before the paint had dried

she lay there
on her stomach
unable and not wanting to move
her mouth tasted of his seed

the welts on her ass were beginning to turn from
red to purple
her flower still vibrated from the incredible
pounding he had given her
if she tried to stand right now her wobbly legs
would not support her

lying next to her
one arm is draped over her back.
doing that thing he always does
tracing the word "mine" on her tailbone with his
middle finger
the other fingers dusting her skin
just along for the ride

barely blinking
eyes like content little suns poking through dark
mascara clouds
she is broken
yet whole at the same time
and she belongs to him

my strong hand

it was such a casual
comfortable conversation
filled with easy banter
until

I said hand
on throat
and you
oh, and you

I could hear you reel
your breath back in
that tiny wind that told so much
of what you desire

the sound of surprise
and recognition
as your heart skipped
then pounded

my strong hand needs
to help you become that
the heart skipping a beat girl
and your pearly flesh needs a bruise

bring your scent home to me

three
powerful words
which
can seemingly show only vulnerability
carry
with them a subtle gift
demonstrating
strength and courage

I miss you

I can watch over you from afar
and with those words my reassurances are
delivered
without naming your vulnerabilities
and the reminder to come
leave your scent on my pillows

reprieve

I need you to beat me

a simple message that required no further
explanation

an understanding
reached without ever negotiating
words or conditions

like a child laying a strap in the hands of the
headmaster
implied admission of transgressions

discipline
not punishment
a reprieve
not a pardoning
more a stay of execution

his loving brutality
dispensed
tears
act as witness
release
not escape

temporary relief
from her burdens
shackles loosened
and tightened
simultaneously

fist full of you

I've had this itch
all day long
a mental scratch is needed
and a fist full of your hair

nape of neck
handful of hair
held in a vice
that is my fist

your gasp igniting
the pyre that grew
in the mind of my loins
the longing for that tug

like reins your tresses
I control your primal urges
steering and guiding you
driving us to that place

pulling you towards
my soft and my bite
you yield and melt
from the pleasure and pain

you, and I, and pillow talk

I know almost to the minute
how long it has been since last I awoke
face between your shoulders kissing
the place where **X** marks the spot that makes you
purr like a kitten

your perfume of sleep and sex
is worn only for me
though you sometimes wear it long into the day
just to let others know what contentment smells
like

and how is it
that your flesh always tastes of salt and honey
making me lick my lips
after each mouthful of you

I think we need some more pillow talk lover...

afraid

her heart was pounding
beating so hard it choked her throat
filled her head with pain

yet she ran on

she stumbled and fell
gravel grinding into her hands and knees
little droplets of crimson encircling the stony
imprints
she could barely stand

yet she ran on

pain enveloped her
muscles cramping
bruises and scrapes searing
she could barely breathe

yet she ran on

she tripped again
her face crashing into the ground
lightning filled her head
blood trickled from her lips

yet she ran on

it was not what she was running from
that had her so afraid
no
it was what she was running towards

yet she ran on...

three magic words

say it Sir
please
say the magic words

you haven't earned them yet kitten
his hands so tight on her hips
there would be purple reminders of it tomorrow
cock thrusting so deep
her hands were knotted in folds of the sheets
pulling her face into the bed

please Sir
she pleaded again
say the magic words

show me you deserve them
by gripping my cock with your cunt
like it's a greedy little fist
then maybe I will say it

she squeezed with all her might
biting down on a mouthful of cotton
as he plunged deeper
making her want to cum so bad
she growled like a caged animal

I fucking hate you
her muffled response

that's what I wanted to hear
he growled in return
crashing his load into her

now kitten
you may cum for me

worthless fucking whore

like a blonde bruise

you're pretty today.

she went from smiling to staring at the floor in
record time
compliments, they never sit well with the ones
who long for them the most
vanity wrapped in a tortilla of insecurities
each bite leaving a bitter taste
more lime juice next time
maybe...

he placed a finger under her chin
lifting her face so their eyes would meet

pretty, like a blonde bruise.

her smile returned
comfortable with the distinction
the clarification

she took his hand
kissing his palm
like a battlefield prayer
the blessing of a weapon

creativity is sexy,
come add some pretty to me...

fuck me with a whisper...

fuck me with a word, she said
one perfect word

fuck me with your mind, she said
simultaneously benevolent and cruel

fuck me with your voice, she said
a sound like rocks slowly breaking

but, most of all, she said
fuck me with a whisper...

simplicity

I'm in a mood.
You're in a mood.
We had words,
not the pretty ones we usually devour.

Brooding.
All day.
The both of us,
and we need to remember why we are.

I hold the solution.
Pure simplicity.
What we need,
is what I will take from you.

No performance art.
No spectacular apparatus.
Just the pure simplicity,
of my hands.

One look and you take position.
Face down and ass up on our bed.
One strong hand between your shoulder blades,
pinning you firmly in place.

Oh, how perfect the simplicity.
Of making us of one mind again.
By leaving handprint tattoos on your ass,
until you soak the sheets with tears.

lightning

his fingers
quietly
slid beneath
lightly tracing her spine
deliver electricity
charging her mind
her body
with a storm front of emotion

simultaneously
tensing
and relaxing

nothing
makes her feel more

protected
at risk of exposure
than his lightning

what I hear when she says Sir

when she says Sir
I hear the mutual respect we have for each other
from her perspective

it's not an honorific title that I want
or desire

it's not my name

what I hear
is thank you
for being my trusted companion

**between your shoulders lies a sleeping
dragon**

your eyelashes
scratch the pillowcase
an imperceptible sound
yet the dragon stirs

on your side
one wing over you
talon nestled
between breasts

the other
underneath
greedy talon
between thighs

I
your protector
you
my treasure

quietly
savoring
rhythmic fire
between shoulder blades

that color looks good on you

the blush pink on your cheeks
when I tell you something that you needed to
hear

the rose welt like the head of an asp
after the bite of a riding crop

the plum tint of a fresh hand print
on your ass or your throat

the prism of iridescent purple, green and yellow
as the memory of a bruise tells its last tale

the brightness of your ruby lips
flushed with excitement and anticipation

the dark red chasms that remain
long after the rope has been untied

that color looks good on you

so
let us
you and I
choose your wardrobe for the day

make me take it from you

I don't want easy
you on a silver platter
with a bow on your ass
not an option

make me work for it
make me earn your gifts
your body
your submission

get all switchy on me
so I can demonstrate my power
you need it
I need it

so
unbuckle my belt
let it lose
with a hand on my hip
listen to that last moment
of your control

take my belt
and drape it around your neck

smile that bratty smile
then run

fast

make me take it from you lover
make me take it all
I don't want it easy
nor do you

party dress

stand there in that cute little party dress
fidgeting and staring at your Mary Jane's
hands clasped behind your back
that crooked grin almost protection

soon
your lips will be a bright red smudge across your
mouth and cheeks
your mascara will run down your face like tiny
black lightning bolts
your hair will be knotted and ruffled
your pretty dress will be torn and tossed on the
floor

soon
you will look up at me with those tear filled eyes
and wordlessly scream...

take me, break me.

morning sex

when she ran her tongue across his lips
his mustache tasted of coffee and smoke
and the honey freshly harvested from between
her thighs

fingers rested
over her pounding heart
soft now
unlike the fire that they burned with before
so she mused
on how this began
how he had called her by her secret name
a name that made her feel both vulnerable and
understood

she traced that name
into the sweat on his ink stained shoulder
newly broken nail dragging on his skin

he smiled
the drying blood on his back creaking
as he drew her close
moving her to let loose a happy sigh

after all
morning was long from over

**all this talk about hair pullin' has me in a
fuckin' tizz...**

Yeah,
you heard me right ya bastard,
all this talk about hair pullin' has me really
worked up!

I'm in a fuckin' tizz if ya hadn't noticed,
and I want,
no,
need,
you to take care of this pussy,
and beat my ass,
maybe choke me while you're at it.

And you better fuckin' tease me,
before you hurt me,
'cause I know,
and you know,
there won't be much of me left,
yeah,
my mind will be a blur of happy hurt,
when you're finished.

So,
muthafucker...

grab a fist-full of my hair,
and when I scream,
suffocate me,
with your vicious mouth,
rub my pussy lips,
with the head of your cock,
bite my shoulder 'till you feel bone,
push my face,
against the wall,
holding me there,
while you fuck me hard,
balls slappin' my clit hard.

Then,
after you fill me with cum,
please,
finish what you started,
with your strong hand,
like fire on my ass,
my thoughts,
slipping loose from my control,
at least for now,

yeah,
I'm in quite a tizz,
because of you...

on subtlety and Domination

you and I,
in our waking moment,
cheek to cheek,
my morning face,
sandpaper on your velvet skin,
I press and pull,
and thousands of tiny razors,
release your first,
sigh of the day.

The subtle act of submission and Domination,
wherein we renew our bond to each other,
pledging commitment and companionship,
without speaking a word.

themed writing

twenty days of pillow notes

The Choke

Fists holding fast to handfuls of your hair,
my cock pushed forcefully into your mouth and
down your throat,
and the sound of the choke.

"Where would you like me to deliver the goods
this time lover"?...

The Wetness

Ass pushed against my hips, the mass of my
desire nestled in your crack,
as a morning ritual of awakening begins with my
knee lifting your leg to let my fingers rest firmly
on your clit producing a sleepy moan from you,
followed shortly by a happy sigh,

as I push the head of my cock into the wetness.

The Words

Your mouth holds many wonders, spilling forth
to please and provoke me, greedy girl who gets
her way when I get mine.
And oh, such delicious aural enticement, you
willingly offer to me, knowing that my cock gets
a very special kind of hard, when you look over
your shoulder and whisper the words,

"Please, fuck my ass"...

The Mark

Somewhere on your skin, there will always be a skillfully placed note, from me to you, almost undetectable to anyone else. A fingerprint, my signature on our contract, and you will smile softly, when you see the mark,

the reminder that you belong with me, and to me.

The Hurt

When your cacophonous mind, has the need for
structure and discipline, and your eyes are
pleading please, break me, take me, own me, the
most loving thing I can do, is respond,

and bring you the hurt.

The Promise

Along with your submission, there comes what
could be construed, as an obligation, whereas, it
is actually an opportunity, for both of us to grow.
It is always, in my best interest, to hold, your best
interest, in a very safe place,

and the promise to do that, is no obligation in
the least.

The Understanding

We have a shared experience, a conscious effort to connect, not only because we need to, because we want to, and from this, there is balance. The dynamic, that provides us the capacity, to hear each other, along with the understanding,

to embrace the message being shared.

The Struggle

Pinned against the wall, by the hair I hold in one
hand, and the wrist I hold in the other, you
punch and slap, as if a black eye, or a sting on my
cheek, will in any way, change the outcome, of
what I have planned. You will always, lose the
struggle, that you invited, with your need,

yet you always win.

The Trust

Is it lust, sparking that fire in you lover, the flame
that lights up your face and radiates in your eyes,
no matter what I choose, to feed your hunger?
Of course, she replied, with a smile like fireworks
exploding, but even more,

it's the trust.

The Moment

The anticipation of impact, that feeds the desires
and expectations, of the Us that is you and me,
thrives on the certain uncertainties, to be
delivered when together we, achieve arrival at the
event horizon. More than the sting, and the heat,
and the glow, is the feeling of true connection,

when we are as one, in the moment.

The Comfort

Her body vibrates from the low rumble of his breathing, his waking growl, that's what she calls it, and she pushes herself even deeper into his hold. His arms tighten around her, an involuntary need to keep her safe and near, and she releases a gasp, and a sigh, then a smile,

from the comfort of it all.

The Surrender

He watched and waited, with serene patience,
from the very onset, knowing what she was
hiding, locked in her heart. His worthwhile
investment just, to witness her discovery, of her
beautiful submission when,

she realized the surrender.

The View

She stood beside him, glowing with a beauty
which she had never imagined, could ever
emanate from within, her, self-imposed exile. He
basked in the radiance, created by her, trust and
fear, of stepping into the liberation and
submission, so long sought. He only wished, he
could show her,

how spectacular the view, from his eyes.

The Primal

Biting, clawing, loving, punching, mating,
nuzzling, tasting, smelling, devouring...
Predator and prey, igniting the very air
surrounding them, with the intensity of,

the primal connection, their unbreakable bond.

The Eyes

She liked to pretend, that she wasn't aware, in the very least, that he was watching her. Looking off in another direction, as if in deep reflection, but it was always a ruse, to steal the warmth of his view, for just another moment. She felt so adored, when she coyly let her bad girl out to play, knowing full well he wasn't fooled, and yet was rewarded with, that *you are my good girl* grin of his,

the eyes, truly are, windows to this kitten's soul.

The Praise

She sat kneeling, like a hungry pauper, arms
outstretched with hands cupped, waiting to be
nourished. Her greedy need for it, made the
absence almost unbearable, reminding her of the
protocol required and that,

the praise she longed for, had to be earned,
before he would return her gift.

The Touch

His fingertips seemed, made of pure energy,
when they danced lightly on her skin. She felt
pulses, of electricity, with every contact, every
brush, of his knuckles, across her flesh. She laid
back, closing her eyes, remembering his hands,

longing for the touch, that would ignite her soul
on fire, over and over, again and again

The Confessional

She drops to her knees for so many reasons. To
give thanks, to ask forgiveness, to renew and
refresh the bond that they share that is so dear to
both of them. It is theirs, it is sacred, and she
always returns to that place in her mind,

the confessional that is his voice in her ear,
where she finds true absolution.

The Patience

He finds it charming, her push, and pull, and fight, and bite, that side of her that asks for his attention, to her details. She is complexity, and simplicity, a challenge requiring many things of him. So, the greatest gift he can present to her, his continued evolution and understanding, is delivered with a ribbon and a bow each day,

the patience he affords her, so she may grow at her own pace.

The List

He had, over time, subtracted and added, what seemed most important and necessary, to his agenda for happiness. Yet, his painstaking efforts, had borne only disappointment. Then one day, he looked deeply into her eyes, and found the beautiful imperfection that he really sought. And with that he accepted her gift,

the list that she had unknowingly written for him, long before they had ever met.

tandem series

: in partnership or conjunction

tandem

I dream of your wet
mind and form as clay to mold
as my hands work you

Need me
knead me
form me in your imagine
you are the god on the alter
Bend me to your will alone

How to not break you
as I bend you to my will
and imagine what to make

tandem deux

He looked at her,
not thru her like everyone else in her life did.
He looked at her and saw who she truly was.

Her vulnerability falling away,
like a veil of invisibility she had worn through
eternity.
Safe for the first time in a very long time.

She could, at last, breathe.
Release.
Exhale.
Inhale his scent, his touch, his words, his truth.

He also needed these,
things that he had never known or had forgotten.
She looked at him and saw who he truly was.

A man.
Her man.
And she, His.

tandem trois

She woke, groggy
sore muscles fueling memories of him
of the proceeding night

She felt every eye,
upon her as she attempted to walk normally or sit
comfortably.
Her rose tattoos already turning yellow and green
around the edges.

She felt his hands still upon her.
Strong fingers digging deep within her tender
white flesh.
Hot breath tracing everywhere his digits
connected with her skin.

They were companions who,
found solace in sex-as-a-sport passion and other
dark proclivities.
Last night she requested that he both fuck her
like a whore and leave marks of shame and
beauty.

They both left it there...in the delicious physical
realm.
Not ready,
not able
for more.
Two broken souls putting the physical pieces
together
Together.
But leaving the rest of the work for another day,
another time,
another lover.

tandem quatre

She was ready to unwrap her mental,
bandages and witness the recovery.
Yet her heart remains in a lockbox of its own
design.

Shattered & scared,
tormented by the voices,
and faces,
of the past;
hands holding her underwater,
lungs screaming for air.

Waves of unworthy crashed in to,
wash away all signs of hope.
The box like Pandora's plague and despair.

Then, suddenly, surprisingly
a hand shot out of nowhere
of thin air.
A hand attached to a strong arm,
fingers encircling her flailing wrist
pulling her to the surface.
To the waiting sunlight.

tandem cinq

I can taste your words in my mouth.
So cold and metallic like blood on,
my tongue after they slap my thoughts.

Is your silent indifference better than this? Your
words of hate doled out
in rapid succession
like the blows of a prize fighter.

I dredge those words out of you knowing of the
pain you cling to.
And that pristine sense of isolation you,
mistakenly view as your armor and mine.

I won't back down but refuse to strike back
Hit me, slap me, punch me in the gut
Break my nose, break a rib with your words
For whatever you say, I know you're hurting
more.

Black mascara tears, like lightning bolts run.
From my word bruised eyes,
and there is no walk of shame.

short stories

No kitten, leave them on...

She came through the door like a blonde tornado...

Some days it was all she could do to hold herself together past the threshold, and she already had one pump in her hand when she looked up and saw him there. He had that serene look, the one that just said let me take away the troubles of your day.

It made her melt...

He could be so gentle,
it was his way most of the time,
until he wasn't,
and she needed that too.

He knelt down with one hand on her hip to steady her and removed the other pump. Shoes dangling from his fingers he took her by the hand and led her into the bedroom. He motioned her to sit on the end of the bed while he went and started a bath.

She was reaching up to pull the pins from her hair when his hand stopped her with a grip of her wrist. He placed his hands on her shoulders pulling her up against him. He smelled so sweet, sweat and cologne, her face nuzzling deep into his shoulder.

He reached around and unzipped her tight black skirt, letting it drop to the floor with no ceremony. Then nimble fingers worked loose every one of the tiny buttons on her blouse. Another unceremonious plop on the floor.

Sliding the tips of his fingers under the straps of her bra, oh she let out a sigh now. Hands one at a time caressing her shoulders as he worked the lace off her ample breasts. God how she loved when he did that, made her feel dirty and adored at the same time. Cupping her breasts in his hands like he was testing them for balance and road wear. Thumbs pushing her nipples to the side with a firm yet tender stroke. She sighed and trembled, butter in his hands.

When his hands finally slid down her hips to catch on the edges of her panties, he looked up and held her dark eyes for the longest time in his gaze. Her day did slip away in the blue ocean that reflected back at her.

And then she was naked.
Exposed.
Standing before him with nothing left but her dark rimmed glasses.

She moved to take them off, and he took hold of her wrist before she could complete the thought.

"No kitten, leave them on"...

He moved to the bathroom to shut off the hot bubbly water that had now filled the tub. Returning she found him also naked.

Yet he was never exposed.

Placing his hands on her shoulders, a signal to lower herself to her knees. She complied and took his hard cock into her hands ready to swallow it as if it would give her the air she needed to breathe easy. This is how she let the cares of the day go.

One of her ways...

Being his cock whore.
Took away her grace.
And gave it back.

Sustaining her.

Something of Substance

She surveyed the room like a panther looking for the weakest gazelle to cull from the herd. This, her pattern, her form, had just one function. It provided her with a lucrative income and in return supplied the total detachment she craved to maintain a bubble of isolation.

Yet tonight, tonight the skeletons with suits hanging off them held not even the slightest appeal. Leave them for the other whores to feed on she thought to herself. I need something of substance tonight, yet tonight.

Before that unwanted desire had time to register as uncomfortable she saw him. Sitting in an overstuffed leather chair. One leg crossed over the other, a book that was too old to be welcome here perched on his knee. A confident and casual slouch that almost had him lost from the room, sinking into the chair as if it were a subtle camouflage.

As she approached it became apparent that his dark grey suit was like a second skin, vest holding up a scarlet tie that still hugged his neck even though it was long past the time of disregard. Crooked arm supporting his head with a hand wrapped thoughtfully around his chin and mouth. Thought filled, he was lost behind glasses that rested halfway down his nose.

She sat down across from him, seemingly waking the man from his faraway place as he grinned just a little. She danced with him, with words, and he in turn played her music, with his. And when she felt it was time she offered him her gift, not free of course, yet a gift just the same.

His eyes locked onto hers for the longest moment, and she shuddered. An odd response and she pushed past it so not to acknowledge. He nodded agreement and they drifted upstairs to her hotel room.

Once inside her room he turned and held her by the shoulders and placed the softest kiss on her forehead. Then those same hands pushed her hard against the wall and she gasped with surprise. A hand moved to her throat and pinned her in place.

No words needed to be exchanged, his eyes shared the script of the next part of their story.

She knew instinctively not to move, and somehow wanted this, needed this. Her breath came in slow strained gasps as he took her hand and placed it on the front of her blouse. She unbuttoned it, breasts falling out as it slid from her shoulders. He gave her just enough slack to undress, just enough. Then she pushed her skirt and panties over her hips and let them hit the floor.

There was no ceremony, no pretense, just his fingers shoved into her. His eyes locked on hers as if he could see into her very soul, and he was claiming possession of it along with her body. She tried to moan but it stuck under his hand in her throat. Her eyes teared as he finger fucked her hard, so hard, and she wanted to scream, and breath, and cum.

His grip tightened just a little just as his fingers jammed in so deep she felt like she might actually break apart. And she came, knees buckling, and he leaned in to support her with his chest against hers, like nothing she had ever dreamed of before.

As she started to collapse he took her into his arms and laid her on the bed, where she drifted off into a place, oh such a place, of serine delight. He undressed and slid into bed next to her and she drifted off to sleep.

When he woke in the morning he found 5 one hundred dollar bills and a note on the nightstand:

Thank you for taking my gift,
something I never knew I had within me to give.
You saw me as something of substance,
and I will be forever grateful for the gift you gave
in return.

Goddess

He was leaning against a pole in the dungeon,
arms crossed and dressed for battle.

Waiting to watch her work.

No, work isn't the correct description.
That would be like saying waves work to pound
rocks into sand on a barren seashore on some
long forgotten island. Her dance doesn't take
work; it just flows with its own rhythm.

She sidled up next to him, looking like an evil
gypsy in her corset and flowing skirt.
"When you wear those leather pants it makes me
more dangerous," she laughed.
"Lucky for him," he replied with a grin.

Music was pulsing in the air as she secured her
willing victim by the wrists to the rack. She
pulled his ass out with a tug on his hips. Like a
marksman loading a clay pigeon into the launch.
Prepping the target before taking aim and silently
saying "pull".
She always entered her own trance, letting the
sounds wash over her, pulling forth her unique

brand of sadism. He liked being a part of it by osmosis. Something that she responded to as well. Energy creating energy. Fission and reaction from a crash of sorts.

Working the boy with her floggers, warming him up. The dance started. Her dance.

When she advanced to the paddle, then the dragon tail, that's when it truly began. Her demons came out to exorcise his, this willing victim. This leather beast liked to bite flesh and he cried out several times. *Fuck! Oh, Fuck!* But she just curtsied and continued. Bowing like a conquering hero returning from a strange land with gifts plundered for the one on the throne.

A single tail in each hand when she decided to move the coming apocalypse up by a day or two. With graceful arcs the tails singled in on their prey. The boy flinched and danced on the tips of his toes, shuffling weight back and forth.

"Oh God" he cried out.

And then the world stopped...

She walked up behind him jerking his head back,
and with a deliberate clarity her words rang
through the din.

"There is no God here, only a Goddess"

Her laughter bubbled out and pulled her back
into her space, he was just along for her ride.

After all, it was the boy who paid for the ticket...

The Stall

She had been thinking,
and dreaming,
all day,
of him.

Distracting his words are,
little traces of sexual lightning,
residual thunderclaps,
her mind and body wanting a full on storm.

She finally succumbed to the need,
checking every stall for occupants,
she was alone,
with her desires.

Clawing hands lifted her skirt,
no time for pleasantries,
fingers sliding in and taking her attention,
she didn't hear the creak of the door.

He shoved her face against the cold metal,
she moved reactionary,
placing a foot on the porcelain,
and grabbing her ass to spread and receive him.
She knew he would find her,

longed for this moment,
his breath hot on her neck,
him thrusting in hard.

Her breathy grunts echoed,
his rang in her ear,
he exploded inside,
and he held her up as knees buckled.

He spun her around,
finishing with a kiss,
"Nice to finally meet you," he said,
"What fucking took you so long"? she whispered.

A Collar of Pearls

She was struggling to reach the zipper when his hands slid onto her waist, cinching her gown into place, then slowly confining her form with a tug. Beautiful she was, swathed in red silk and fiery tresses. Resting his chin on her shoulder from behind, he gazed at their reflection, then surprised her, extending his open hand. Her eyes glided down his arm, past the cuff and link, to a sparkling gift. A pearl necklace.

Before you may wear this, he told her, you need to let it become what it truly is.

She turned to look upon him, his tuxedo darkest black, tie hanging like a cavalier banner on a field of crisp white cotton. She knelt before him and unzipped his trousers. Taking his cock in her hands, she wrapped the pearls around his shaft and balls ever so gently. Then, placed his head in her mouth and began the transformation. Letting her spit roll down onto the tiny orbs, she slid them against his flesh, holding on with both hands. She had known without being told just what he had asked of her, to make this trinket into a collar of pearls.

In spite of her greed to taste every last drop, she let his cum fill her mouth and run back out. Down her chin and hands, coating each bead with his. When she finished he took her new adornment and placed it around her neck. As he fastened it, he spoke a sentiment that made tears well up in her eyes. No matter what you wear kitten, you belong to me.

Ritual

bubbly they called her,
the cute blonde with the angelic laugh,
how's that new puppy?
water cooler chit-chat,
even the copier guy treated her like she might
break,
they all saw only,
what they wanted to see,
her grace,
surface not scratched,
pristine,
like a new penny.
it was nothing short of unpredictable,
that the two of them would share something so
primal,
but she noticed him,
noticing her,
looking right into her dark soul,
exposing her only,
and quietly to himself,
the man with the rough edges and nice suits.

they exchanged hungry covert glances for weeks,
the only one who looked at her like she was
lunch and dessert,
she wanted to be on his menu,

longed to be,
as the others passed by,
oblivious to her needs,
her twisted offerings,
he knew,
oh, somehow he knew.

so when Friday came,
and the lights were turning down,
she was on her way out last,
when she summoned up her breath,
held it firm as she opened his office door,
finding him lost in thought,
of which there was no real need.

he sat back with that knowing smile of his,
oh what a bastard he was for understanding her
so,
and spoke not a word as she unbuckled his belt,
tugging his pants open to expose his greedy cock,
then turning so his hands could raise her dress up
around her waist,
panties long removed after soaking through
before lunch had arrived,
she sat down on his lap spreading legs wide,
his hands moving around to grab her knees,
wider still yes,

then pushing the head of his cock against her wet
folds.

before she could barely let out a sigh,
his arm wrapped around her pulling tight,
smashing her breasts and chaffing her nipples,
he started to rub her clit with his head,
fingertips lightly touching her wet lips,
driving her wild,
she had been building this in her mind for weeks,
So it didn't take long,
no, for her first round to squirt out and cover his
shaft.

he didn't give her a moment to breath,
before popping it into her,
his arm now moving up to her shoulder,
pulling her down to impale her on him,
oh, she wiggled her ass to drop in tight,
hearing him sigh in acknowledgement,
how did he know what she had longed for,
to be used like this,
to use him like this.

she placed her hands on his knees for leverage,
and started to grind and ride,
he held firmly onto her waist just grazing her
hips,
a hand floating to grapple with her bouncing

breasts,
or tug on her clit,
until he started to fill her up,
then fingers slid into her mouth to silence her
moans,
she bit down on him as she came again,
him laughing,
one last squeeze of her tits.

his cum mixed with hers,
was beginning to run down her legs as she
walked to the elevator,
heading home and feed the puppy.

this,
was going to become a new Friday night ritual...

Anything

"So what are you needing today," he asked,
"want anything special"?
"I do want something special," she replied, "no
negotiations, surprise me, with anything."

She was bent over a large butcher's block.
Wrists tightly bound to its legs, the edges biting
into her soft flesh.
Legs spread wide, tied with her toes just off the
floor.

She watched as he placed several items on the
counter, to entice and frighten her.
It worked, she was trembling a bit.
A riding crop, a blindfold and a bowl of ice.
Followed by the sound of his belt, sliding loose
of his jeans.

The blindfold, removing any last hope of
foretelling.
She waited, and waited.
Then it suddenly, began.
Searing pain and surprise, as he shoved the first
ice cube in her ass.

She barely had chance to shiver, when the crop
took its first bite.
Her ass was a tiny battleground, of heat and cold.
More bites, more bites.
Then, the second ice cube.

He used his belt tip like a single tail, the back of
her legs started to burn.
Welts forming fast, little red love bites.
He then folded it in half, and hungrily went for
her ass.
Just after, the third ice cube...

Wrapped in a blanket and his arms,
her tear filled voice said,
"Thank you for *anything*,
it means *everything*" ...

About the author

HL37 writes erotic poetry and short stories that capture the BDSM lifestyle as seen through his eyes. When he is not pushing words around with a pen, he can be found making whips, riding his motorcycle affectionately known as "the big red bitch" and planning his next tattoo.

Made in the USA
Monee, IL
18 May 2024

58596305R00056